THE THREE BEARS

ILLUSTRATED BY

F. Rojankovsky

GOLDEN PRESS
Western Publishing Company, Inc.
Racine, Wisconsin

This is one of the Little Golden Books which
bring children the best of the world's folk tales
with fresh illustrations by outstanding children's
book artists. Feodor Rojankovsky's pictures for
books published in this country and in Europe
have endeared him to children the world over.

Thirty-Seventh Printing, 1978

Copyright 1948 by Western Publishing Company, Inc.
All rights reserved. Produced in U.S.A.

Once upon a time there were three bears—
a great big papa bear, a middle-sized mama
bear, and a wee little baby bear.

They lived in a little house in the forest.

And they had three chairs—a great big chair
for the papa bear, a middle-sized chair for the
mama bear, and a wee little chair for the baby
bear.

And upstairs there were three beds—a great
big bed for the papa bear, a middle-sized bed
for the mama bear, and a wee little bed for the
baby bear.

One morning the mama bear made some
porridge for breakfast.

She filled a great big bowl for the papa bear, a middle-sized bowl for the mama bear, and a wee little bowl for the baby bear.

But the porridge was too hot to eat, so the
three bears went out for a walk in the forest.

That same morning a little girl called Goldi-
locks was walking through the woods.

She came to the three bears' house. And she
knocked on the door, but nobody called, "Come
in." So she opened the door and went in.

Goldilocks saw the three chairs. She sat in the great big chair. It was too hard. The middle-sized chair was too soft. The baby chair was just right—but it broke when she sat on it.

Now Goldilocks spied the porridge.

"I am hungry," she said.

So she tasted the porridge.

The porridge in the big bowl was too hot.

The porridge in the middle-sized bowl was
too cold. The porridge in the wee little bowl
was just right—so she ate it all up.

Then Goldilocks went upstairs and tried the beds.

The great big bed was too hard.
The middle-sized bed was too soft.

But the wee little bed was oh, so nice! So
Goldilocks lay down and went to sleep.

Then home through the forest and back to
their house came the three bears—the great big
bear, the middle-sized bear, and the wee little
baby bear.

The moment they stepped into the house,
they saw that someone had been there.

"Humph!" said the papa bear in his great big
voice. "Someone has been sitting in my chair!"

"Land sakes!" said the mama bear in her middle-sized voice. "Someone has been sitting in *my* chair."

"Oh dear!" cried the baby bear in his wee little voice. "Someone has been sitting in *my* chair, and has broken it all to bits."

Then they all looked at the table.

"Humph," said the papa bear in his great

big voice. "Someone has been tasting my porridge."

"And someone has been tasting *my* porridge," said the mama bear.

"Someone has eaten *my* porridge all up,"
said the baby bear sadly.

Then up the stairs went the three bears, with

a thump thump thump,
and a trot trot trot, and a skippity-skip-skip.
(That was the wee little tiny bear.)

"Humph," said the papa bear in his great big voice. "Someone has been sleeping in my bed!"

"And someone has been sleeping in *my* bed," said the mama bear.

"Oh, dear!" cried the baby bear in his wee little voice. "And someone has been sleeping in *my* bed, and here she is right now!"

Goldilocks opened her eyes and she saw the
three bears.

"Oh!" said Goldilocks.

She was so surprised that she jumped right
out of the window and she ran all the way home.
And she never saw the house in the forest again.

14 DAY FREE TRIAL

THE FOUR WONDERFUL WORLDS OF
WALT DISNEY

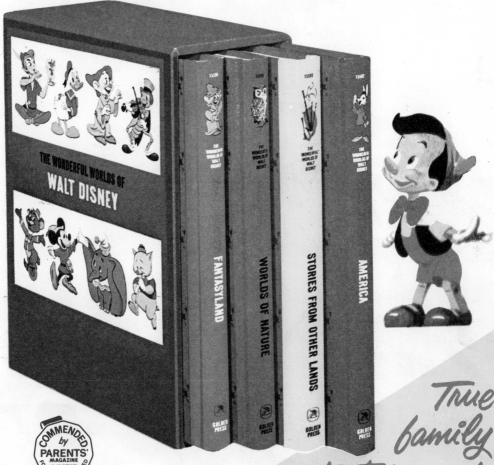

True family entertainment

BACK BY POPULAR DEMAND!
OVER 2 MILLION DELIGHTED CUSTOMERS

* ✱ 4 beautiful volumes
* ✱ 64 magical stories
* ✱ Over 1,000 pages
* ✱ FREE Disney Poster

AT LAST, into your home comes the magic of the greatest story teller of our time—64 of Walt Disney's greatest film stories are assembled in permanent book form—for the delight of your entire family! And you can examine them in your own home for fourteen days free. This enchanting collection of the young in heart comes in four sumptuous, giant-sized volumes…7½"x10½"… over 1,000 pages in full color…in a handsome slipcase. In addition, you will also receive FREE a large Disney poster just for examining this set of books.

FANTASYLAND. You'll go adventuring with Cinderella, the Ugly Duckling, Snow White, the Sleeping Beauty, Peter and the Wolf, and ten other favorite Disney characters—all brought to life in words and glowing color!

WORLDS OF NATURE. Real worlds more amazing than any fairy tale: *The Living Desert, Secrets of Life, The African Lion, The Vanishing Prairie*—plus two beloved stories, *Perri* and *Bambi*. Color photographs from the original Disney films are reproduced on quality paper.

AMERICA. *The Uncle Remus* stories . . . tales such as *Johnny Appleseed* and *Davy Crockett*, stories such as *The Shaggy Dog* and *The Flying Car* . . . excursions with Polly-anna and Old Yeller . . . stories the whole family will enjoy.

STORIES FROM OTHER LANDS. Fourteen of the most delightful Walt Disney creations you've thrilled to on the screen—*Stories from Other Lands, Swiss Family Robinson, Sword in the Stone, Robin Hood, Alice in Wonderland, 101 Dalmatians*, and eight more.

. DETACH AND MAIL THIS POSTPAID CARD TODAY!

Golden Press, Dept. T49
175 Community Drive
Great Neck, New York 11025

Please send me **THE FOUR WONDERFUL WORLDS OF WALT DISNEY** for free 14-day examination. I understand that I can return the four volumes to you without obligation within 14 days, if I am not delighted with them. If I decide to keep them you will bill me at the low price of just $4.99 a month for five months (a total of only $24.95). A small charge will be added to my first invoice for postage, handling and local sales tax. I understand that the FREE POSTER (one per family) is mine to keep even if I return the books.

Name_____

Address_____

City_____ State_____ Zip_____

Parent's Signature_____

The cost of credit is included in the price quoted for the goods and services.
All orders are subject to credit approval of Golden Press Shopper's Service.

AVAILABLE BY MAIL ORDER ONLY.